How I Saved My Friend Jesus

Peter Krause

ISBN 979-8-88685-476-3 (paperback)
ISBN 979-8-88685-477-0 (digital)

Christian Faith Publishing
832 Park Avenue
Meadville, PA 16335
www.christianfaithpublishing.com

Printed in the United States of America

I dedicate this story to my friends in the EfM Group and the congregation of St. John's Episcopal Church in Johnson City, Tennessee.

Many thanks for the support to find my way back to the Lord. Without their help, this book would have never happened!

FOREWORD

Some Thoughts about Time Traveling

Since the paradox of time is so important, I would like to take this opportunity to explain this phenomenon to you, the reader of my story.

What is a time paradox?

Case 1. Let's assume that something like time traveling would be possible, and we could travel back into the past. Let us now imagine that a time traveler would somehow prevent your mother and father from ever meeting, falling in love, and marrying. Then it is possible that you would never be born because your parents never met, which would mean you would not exist in the present time from which the time traveler started.

Case 2. Let's assume that a time traveler killed Adolf Hitler during World War I when he was a soldier. This means World War II would never have happened, and the whole of history would be different.

Case 3. Let's assume that a volunteer who traveled with the time traveler would stay in the past, which would introduce a person who had never existed there before, and somehow this volunteer would became famous and change history in a way that could be seen in the time from which the time traveler started.

This is always the same kind of story. Therefore, time travel into the past is always dangerous because even an unimportant thing can change the course of history. So it can happen that you have started time travel into the past with a known history (history A), and when you return, you see a changed history (history B). Furthermore, only history B would be known if you asked the people because history A never happened.

HOW I SAVED MY FRIEND JESUS

I am Joshua, a nuclear physicist, astrophysicist, and dedicated Christian. I am a true believer in Christ, His words, and His actions. Like every scientist, I am interested in finding the truth about all the tasks and problems that have challenged me. During my career as a physicist, it has become more important to know whether Jesus was a real person. Finally, I developed an ambitious plan to find out the truth about Jesus's story.

Twelve years before

I consider myself a devoted Christian. I visit Bible classes to deepen my understanding of Scripture. I help in a homeless shelter, in an elder care facility, and in my church congregation to ease and comfort other people's lives. Helping others as a Christian is part of my DNA.

This is one side of my daily life. The other is my job as a nuclear physicist working in a research center for nuclear physics and astrophysics. I got a PhD in each field. With the knowledge in both fields, my colleagues and I found some essential new laws of physics, which helped me solve some of the time-travel problems I faced in this story.

My special field is time in space and the possibility of time travel. The time phenomenon in space has always fascinated me because there is no absolute time in space. Time depends on gravity, and that means that at different places, the space-time is different as well. We speak about the space-time continuum because we live in three dimensions, and time is the fourth dimension. Time is not independent, and it is because of certain circumstances.

Time indeed passes more slowly if there is something nearby with significant gravity. If you could be at an event horizon of a black hole, time would become zero; it would not exist anymore.

As a result, a higher gravity creates a slower time. As a worst-case scenario, time will change to zero if the gravity is infinite.

In conclusion, time can go faster or slower and even become zero, but it can never be negative. If this is true, time travel into the past should not be possible because nothing has been known to create time that goes backward—until now.

Assume something like a two-dimensional creature, which is challenged by the height of a wall. It would be impossible for this creature to go over the wall because it cannot handle height as a third dimension!

If we could create a gate to the fifth dimension that we could control, then the time-travel problem could be solved.

And how? We all live in a so-called time-space continuum, defined by height, length, width, and time. Now imagine you could put our time-space continuum in a shoebox and assume that there is an infinite number of these shoeboxes based on different heights, lengths, widths, and times as well. The fifth dimension is the container that includes this infinite number of these shoeboxes. Within the fifth dimension, you could jump from your time-space continuum to another just by leaving your time-space continuum and choosing your destination space-time continuum.

In our scientific research group, we found evidence on a sub-atomic level that this might be possible, but the amount of energy needed to send a human through time would exceed the energy of our sun.

The next questions I asked myself were the following:

- Is there anything available that can deliver this amount of energy under controlled conditions?
- Is there some sort of catalyst available that could be used to drastically lower the energy needed?
- Can we create some sort of field as a bridge to the fifth dimension to overcome time?

First Ideas

After a long time of research and consideration, I decided it would be easier to try time travel in a controlled way using the fifth dimension to travel through time. In my imagination, the fifth dimension should be a room with infinite size and infinite times. If I could choose a location, I could see this room during other times; and if I could choose a time, I would see different places at this time.

I had to solve the problem of finding the correct location and the correct time. However, I saw this problem as minor because I could move to every place and time within the fifth dimension. The only thing I needed was a fixed starting point: my time and location in my time-space continuum at the start of my time-travel journey. The real problem was the jump from my fourth-dimension environment into the fifth dimension, which was essential for time travel. The way back seemed easy because I would be in the fifth dimension and could choose a time and location to jump back into my journey's starting time from there. I named this, the most crucial part of the time machine, Dimension Generator, which should transfer me safely into the fifth dimension like a letter in an envelope. The generator would create a fifth-dimensional field around me and keep me safe within the fifth dimension as long as needed.

But all this theoretical thinking was worth nothing until I solved some more important challenges!

Developing such a machine would require a severe amount of money and several coworkers. I realized it would be impossible to find investors for my project. This project was only beyond any investor's imagination. I would have to release the development of a time machine to many more people. I would ruin my reputation as a scientist, lose everything, and find myself in a sanatorium for mental diseases. I decided to find another way to finance my project for all these reasons.

For the same reasons, I could not reveal the real purpose of my project to any of my coworkers, family, and friends. I had to invent two cover stories to camouflage my real intentions. Then how should a reliable test of the generator look? The prototype would disappear from the standard space-time continuum and create a field of the fifth dimension. How could I prove the time machine would work correctly?

The question that bothered me most was "Which time and location should I choose for my time travel?" My Christian faith helped me a lot in answering this question. As a devoted Christian, Jesus's work, life, and death always fascinated me. So the sheer possibility to use my machine to talk with Jesus or even see Him shook my entire body. It was like a shock when I realized what could happen. I was heavily inspired by this idea and began to think about what I need to make this happen.

In Jesus's world, people spoke several languages. These were Latin, old Greek, Hebrew, and Aramaic. To learn these languages fluently would take me a while. The reason for Aramaic was that modern scientists presumed Jesus spoke Aramaic. The problem with learning Aramaic was to find locations in Syria where this language is still spoken.

THE PLANNING

Developing a reliable plan became the base to successfully reach my goal. I prioritized my first ideas and began to think about what I would need to do. These were the problems to solve:

- Find a reliable monetary source to fund the time machine.
- Find cover stories to hide the purpose of the time machine.
- Develop and test the time machine.
- Hide the real reasons for learning four ancient languages.
- Learn Latin, old Greek, Hebrew, and Aramaic.
- Begin extensive Bible studies to be well prepared to find Jesus.
- Start and plan the duration of my journey.
- Improve physical endurance (because in those days, people traveled by foot).
- Find a cover story about my life during my travel in the past.
- Get money for this time.
- Get clothing for this time.
- Choose what kind of food and equipment I should take with me.
- Learn self-defense techniques for self-protection.
- Create a cover story for my disappearance.
- Prevent life-threatening situations on the journey (for example, first aid kit and medications) and make per-

sonal preparations before the travel starts (for example, a will, handling my mail, etc.).

Because of all these challenges, I realized I would need between ten and fifteen years to prepare for my journey. The most significant part would be the development and testing of the time machine. So I began to work on every point on my list.

Find a reliable monetary source to fund the time machine

In the beginning, it was clear that I could not use any known ways to find a funding source for my project. The reasons were obvious, and I did not intend to make my project public, which would have been necessary if I had chosen the usual way to fund my project.

Therefore, I chose the way of creative bookkeeping. The implementation of this process took me a year. Because it was the most critical problem to be solved, it needed special attention. Because of my scientific work and position, I was responsible for a multimillion-dollar budget and realized the following essential steps.

One of the first steps was to establish companies that seemed to operate in the same field as I did and conduct business with these. Officially, these companies were used as service providers for budget controlling, purchasing, and management counseling. The purpose of these companies was to create short-term investment profits from money, and I paid them for their services, the funds for which came from my official project budget. On the other hand, these companies leased rooms, vehicles, and office equipment from us, so the money returned to my official project. Since both costs and profits were managed in subaccounts in my project, there was no difference in cash at the end of the business year. That would have raised the attention and alerted the budget control department.

Find cover stories to hide the purpose of the time machine

My biggest fear was that the real purpose of my project would be revealed to the public. I saw this possibility caused by some gossipy whistleblowers who would try to make headlines, some super curious journalists who would try to find the story of their lifetime, or just unlucky coincidence.

For these reasons, I saw the need to create reliable cover stories that would withstand the questioning of any ordinary audience, including good explanations for more highly educated people and all kinds of law enforcement offices and agencies at the federal level. The last thing I wanted was to deal with some agents or even the government's potential takeover of my project. I was convinced my time machine should never ever be used by any government because of the implications caused by the time paradox.

I had to consider many points when I created my cover story. To cover up the power generation for the time machine was the most complex problem. I had to skip my first idea (to use a nuclear reactor) because of the additional headache it would have caused. I considered it almost impossible to build a nuclear reactor and get the nuclear fuel unnoticed by the authorities and public. I also had to avoid anything that could create nuclear radiation for that exact reason. Finally, I chose windmills for this, which would give my project some sort of green touch. I used huge state-of-the-art iron-air batteries to store the generated energy.

My first cover story was that this location was a development center for modern high-energy batteries to be used in modern decentralized power grids fed by environmentally friendly energy sources like windmills. Using windmills to generate power fitted this story well.

The second cover story was that this location was for the development of a new wireless method of high-energy transportation.

Because of the danger or possibility of changing the history during time travel and the unpredictable outcome of this change, one of my most important requirements was the self-destruction of the time machine and all documents as the last resort to prevent misuse. This included a device (which I implanted in my body) linked to the potential self-destruction unit of my time machine. If the self-destruction unit should be activated, I could deactivate it within five minutes. After five minutes, the time machine would destroy itself, and the implanted device would kill me. Thus, I ensured nothing of my time machine could be revealed and misused.

The location of my time machine was also critical. I chose a windy rural area for many reasons. The place was far away from big cities, which minimized the risk for people and the environment. Then the people in rural areas would be thankful for getting well-paid jobs. Therefore, it would be much easier to forge a worker spirit, which made these employees feel special, and they would be more sacrificial and suspicious of foreigners. That should make it easier to guard the complex. Finally, enough wind generated the necessary energy for the dimension generator to start the time travel.

Develop and test the time machine

This was the most critical part of my plan. As you could imagine, a time machine with a dimension generator was not easy to develop, like a car, a nuclear power plant, an X-ray machine, or a Large Hadron Collider. The dimension generator should open a controlled way to the fifth dimension so that I could go from my fourth dimension to the fifth dimension and return unharmed. As mentioned before, this was necessary to time travel. The fifth dimension includes endless fourth-dimension elements. Reaching the fifth dimension would mean it would only take the work to find the arrival location, time, and date elements. The departure point (the beginning of my trip) was precisely the same location, time, and date where I jumped from my fourth to the fifth dimension. This point would be marked and locked for the way back.

The dimension generator provided only the bridge from the fourth to the fifth dimension. The way back was trivial because a fifth-dimension space always includes the fourth dimension. This means the dimension generator had to produce a fifth-dimensional field like a small bubble. This bubble should cover my time machine and me and be transferred immediately into the fifth dimension.

As expected, the development of the dimension generator needed a lot of time, money, and resources.

Covering the device's real purpose was almost impossible, especially when the first tests were conducted. The question was how I should carry out the test without risking human life or the time machine itself. The problem was that the time machine would disappear immediately because it would jump into the fifth dimension, choose its final time-and-place destination, and stay there forever. Apparently, we had to solve two problems; the first was some sort of autoreturn mode, and the second was a probe that could be used to confirm the destination time and location. Resolving the second problem was easier than expected. The only reliable sources to be used were the star constellations. So we installed special cameras that could make star images at night that we could later use in combination with the unchanged time in the time machine to calculate the date, time, and location at the destination point. The first problem was at least half solved because we had to mark our entry point in the fifth dimension anyway to be used as an exit point back into our time and place. After all, however, we found that there was no difference in principle between the time jump into the past and the last time jump into the future; the procedure was similar.

The installation of a fully automated system for travel time, date, and location had been developed and had become an essential part of the time machine. We recognized the importance of such a system late in the development process. The reason was that no one could know the influence of such travel on the human body and mind. This fully automated time-travel navigator provided the opportunity to be sent back in the event of lost consciousness or serious injuries.

In general, the dimension generator punched a hole into the space-time continuum to reach the fifth dimension. The fifth-dimensional field created this hole within the fourth-dimensional space-time continuum.

When this happened, the entire time machine disappeared out of the fourth-dimensional space-time continuum, leaving a strange noise caused by the vacuum created by its disappearance. At the destination point, all things at the reentry point were pushed away from the time machine and created some kind of small shock wave.

The energy consumption per time jump was gigantic, as was the energy storage for the jump back. Interestingly, the energy needed to force the time machine from the fourth-dimensional space-time continuum into the fifth-dimensional space was given back when we jumped back into the fourth-dimensional space-time continuum.

On a subatomic level, there is a similar effect that's well-known. An electron can jump to a higher energy level in a stable orbit when energy is added to the electron. When the electron jumps back to its former level, the energy used is returned.

From the perspective of the time machine, we stored the energy returned when we reached our destination, a different space-time continuum. The combination of time jumps and time machine was some kind of energy pendulum with a huge energy storage. The advantage was obvious: we could jump time almost immediately without a long wait for energy storage to recharge.

Hide the real reasons for learning Latin,
old Greek, Hebrew, and Aramaic

Learning these four languages was one of my biggest challenges in this project. When I started this, all my buddies and friends who knew me as a devoted Christian thought I had lost my mind. Any of these languages were difficult to learn, but learning four of these was considered insane. I could convince my friends that I was interested in reading the Bible in the original languages for deeper understanding. This was the reason I purchased an intense amount of Bible literature and Bibles in these four languages.

Learn Latin, old Greek, Hebrew, and Aramaic

Learning to speak Latin was the easiest part because the alphabet is familiar and grammar is based on logic. I could find classes everywhere. Hebrew was more difficult to learn. Hebrew is spoken in Jewish communities worldwide, but they use Hebrew letters, which have nothing to do with our alphabet. We had coworkers in Israel willing to support me. I even used this opportunity to visit the Holy Land as a tourist, including the caves of Qumran.

Old Greek and Aramaic were the most difficult languages to learn because they used their own alphabets. Old Greek is not spoken anymore, but I could still learn it now. Aramaic is still in use in some corners of Syria. At least there, I could visit and practice the language with some people.

I started all four languages with online classes and later switched to in-person courses. After four years of intense study, I could speak all four languages fluently. Thus, the main work (learning these languages) was done. However, I had to practice using them until my journey would begin.

Begin extensive Bible studies to be
well prepared to find Jesus

The intense study of the Bible was an obvious thing to do. Both the Old Testament and the New Testament were equally important, and I used all four ancient languages to read original Bible texts for better understanding. As a result of all my studies, I realized I needed to improve my knowledge of the different societies at different places in Jesus's lifetime and their rites and manners. Furthermore, I had to build up some knowledge about geography in these areas, like cities, rivers, and mountains.

Start and plan the duration of my journey

Before I determined the destination, time, and location of my time travel, I collected facts about Jesus's life. Luke 3:23 shows us that Jesus was about thirty when He started ministry (AD 26–30) and was in ministry for three years, placing Jesus's death at AD 29–33. The gospel accounts place the beginning of Jesus's ministry in the countryside of Roman Judea, near the River Jordan. In the New Testament accounts, the main locations of the ministry of Jesus were Galilee and Judea, with activities also taking place in surrounding areas such as Perea and Samaria. Capernaum was the town where Jesus began His ministry and spent most of His time during His earthly ministry.

Based on these facts, I decided to set the destination date to March 20, AD 25. The hour of the day was not critical. The problem with the location was that I needed a solid hiding place for my time machine, something like a cave in an unsettled area. I got the idea of my hiding place from a former visit to the Qumran Caves. I knew these caves would be big enough to hide my time machine, and the area was perfect because almost nobody lived there. The significant disadvantage was that the city of Capernaum was about 160 kilometers away, and I would need eight days to walk from the Qumran Caves to Capernaum. Nevertheless, I saw no other option, so I used this destination location for the time machine, in the middle of the biggest cave.

The duration of my visit to Jesus's time should contain His first appearance in public until His crucifixion. So I ended up with a time frame between four and six years, depending on how early I met Jesus and His disciples. Luckily, I could cover this length easily with my time machine, and I chose a return time that was only two months away from my start time.

Improve physical endurance (because in
those days, people traveled by foot)

I had to improve my endurance because in Jesus's days, people traveled mainly by foot. I hired a personal trainer who could perfectly handle my strict schedule and offered effective training. Over time, my fitness and endurance improved, which was good in many ways. After my stressful job, I found relaxation in this kind of training. I hardened my spirit and body. I wore shoes like Jesus's when I took long-distance walks. In the beginning, this was challenging because these shoes were a type of primitive sandals, which were by far not as comfortable as my sneakers. After some long-distance walks, my feet got used to it. As a nice side effect, I lost a lot of weight, which was not only good for my health. In Jesus's times, only rich people could afford to be fat, and an overweight man traveling by foot would have caused some unwanted attraction. Additionally, the many walks outside gave my skin a nice brown tone, which would help me blend in with the people of Jesus's time even better. The last step was obtaining a full beard, which I let grow because beardless people mainly were Roman soldiers, Roman citizens, and Roman noblemen, and I had no intention to play my role as a Roman. My goal was to blend perfectly into the Jewish society in Judea during Jesus's time.

My cover story about my life during my travel in the past

During my preparations for my time travel, one problem jumped into my head. I would meet and speak with many people asking me about my life and profession. My idea was to pretend to be a holistic healer who had been sent from the headmaster of the University of Alexandria to areas around the Dead Sea and the Sea of Galilee to learn more about how people with different illnesses would be treated. I chose a travel route that Jesus walked several times. After arriving at the port of Joppa, the other stations of my travel were Jerusalem, Jericho, the Dead Sea, along the Jordan River to the Sea of Galilee, Capernaum, Nazareth, Salem, Ephraim, Jerusalem, Joppa, and back to Alexandria.

Get money from this time

The most popular Roman coin in this area used at the time of Jesus's crucifixion was the denarius. This coin was made from silver and was valid in the time 211 BC–244 AD. I purchased some of these coins from a coin retailer and copied them. For this purpose, I used my technical equipment to meet the correct silver alloy. I created a press die that I used to produce the needed number of coins. The aging of the coins was the last step to make them look genuine.

Get clothing for this time

The typical clothing for Jesus at Jesus's times was made from wool, linen, or perhaps animal skins. This clothing was divided into undergarments (an under tunic) and outer garments held together by a cord. The headgear was a large square piece of woolen cloth specially folded and held in place by a cord circlet. The typical footwear was sandals made from leather to protect the feet from burning sand and dampness. I visited some Bible museums to get first impressions. In Israel, I found tailors and shoemakers who recreated these ancient types of clothing with the proper materials. So finally, I had two pairs of sandals, two sets of gray woolen undergarments, two light-brown woolen outer garments, and two headwear made from the same color and material.

*Choose what kind of food and equipment
I should take with me*

The most essential food in Jesus's days was bread. If available, also fruits (like figs, grapes, and melons), nuts, locust, fish, and rarely meat. If pure water was available, it was the preferred drink. Light beer, fruit juice, and wine were also drunk. Travelers used wineskins made from goat hide to store their drinks during the journey. During my stay in Israel, getting all this stuff from different shops in Jerusalem was relatively easy. I got dried fish, figs, nuts, and long-lasting fruits for my trip. So I prepared myself in the best possible way. This included two crossover bags made from goat leather to carry all the stuff. Finally, I decided to store my camping equipment and some bags of freeze-dried food, bottles of water, and tea bags in my time machine because I had no idea about the environmental conditions during the first days at my destination.

Learn self-defense techniques for self-protection

Since I would travel mainly by myself, I realized I had to learn some sort of self-defense techniques. The typical weapons those days were a knife, a sword, or a spear. To get captured and sold as an enslaved person, robbed, or killed was common. So I concluded that learning some sort of martial arts would be necessary. After some investigations, I found Tae Kwon Do and combat hapkido more than suitable for me. So I gave this job to my personal trainer, who managed it, teaching me all necessary defense techniques to fight off perpetrators attacking me with weapons of different kinds. I learned to enjoy these practice classes because I could fight off my stressful situation. After all, there were rare occasions.

Create a cover story for my disappearance

During the many years of time-machine development, I lived three different lives. First was my everyday life, doing my job as a project leader at my work. The second was my secret life, in charge of the time-machine project. The third was my life as a devoted Christian. This life significantly helped me cover the work on the time machine. I could use language learning, Bible studies, travel to certain biblical places, etc. as an excuse to improve my understanding of Scripture. Strangely, this happened because due to this intense work, the world of Jesus slowly became mine. It was like assuming a role of a historical figure and diving into His world. So my friends were not surprised when I told them that I wanted to visit an ancient monastery in Jordan for two months.

During this time, I could not be reached by email or phone. I calculated my trip would not last more than two months. This was the time of my absence, which I told my friends and relatives. This was only a precaution because a time traveler can start a trip at the x time, stay for months and years in the time he chose, and return at the x time plus five minutes. After all, he could choose the time when he returned.

*Prevent life-threatening situations on the journey
(for example, first aid kit and medications) and
make personal preparations before the travel starts
(for example, a will, handling my mail, etc.)*

I was pretty much aware that in Jesus's days, illnesses like leprosy, tetanus, polio, chicken pox, and measles were primarily deadly and that, of course, vaccinations had not yet been invented. In case of an injury combined with an open wound, inflammations were also fatal because antibacterial medication had also not been invented yet. A snakebite was also fatal because an antivenom was not yet developed. This meant even a minimal injury could lead to death. I had to consider all these risks. So I took all the necessary vaccinations as a minimum precaution, took first aid classes, and informed myself in Jordan about the medication that a typical tribe in the desert would use today (for example, which plants they used to treat certain illnesses or injuries). So I collected the entire medical equipment piece by piece, including antivenom for spiders, scorpions, and snakes, which I considered necessary on my trip to Jesus's time.

Personal preparations before the travel starts

I had to think that something could go drastically wrong even under the best circumstances. There was a final remaining risk that I couldn't prevent or exclude. Therefore, I formulated my last will and deposited it with a lawyer, and I gave him written instructions that my will be opened if I did not return within two months of my trip. Of course, I did this at the last possible moment to prevent the leakage of this circumstance.

Last Preparations

Today, after many years of developing the time machine, the main part, and the dimension generator and all other preparations, my time travel to Jesus could finally begin. As the last steps before starting, I arranged my affairs, gave my cat to a cat sitter for approximately two months, informed the postal office that they should store my mail for about two months, and gave the company that took care of my house some last orders. I told my friends and relatives that I would make a two-month trip and that they should not worry about me. Both friends and relatives asked me whether I could be reached via email or cell phone during this time, and I told them no because the monastery I would visit would not allow this.

Over these many years, it was not easy to hide my fast-growing time machine and all the auxiliary equipment necessary to undertake this trip, but I finally made it happen. Nobody else involved in the development of this machine had any idea about its real purpose.

Everything necessary for my trip had been stowed away in cabinets, shelves, and drawers. Emotionally, I had jumped between feeling uncomfortable and excited. I believe Christopher Columbus might have felt like I did when he started his journey to find a new passage to India, not knowing what might lie ahead of him.

My journey begins

Before I started the time machine, I went through the checklist to avoid last-minute problems. The energy heart of my machine had been beating for one year to generate and store all the energy I needed for this time jump. The constant and steady sound of the machine calmed me down. All control lights were green, and the main computer was ready to go. I sat in the control seat, buckled up, and had a final drink of water. After checking the target date, time, and location again, I handed the controls to the main computer and started counting. I closed my helmet during this time. At the end of the countdown, I saw a bright light, and my surroundings disappeared.

My arrival in a time about two thousand
years ago in the Qumran Caves

I can't describe what happened, but the effects I heard and saw were a deep, loud sound of the dimension generator, like the beat of a large drum, then a bright light and, finally, silence. My first thought was that it had gone wrong, but the control panel of the time navigation computer showed me that the expected location and reallocation were the same (31.73 N and 35.46 E), and the actual date and time was also the expected date and time (March 20, AD 25, and it was 2:00 p.m.).

I looked through my window and saw that my environment had changed entirely from the inner side of a concrete building to a cave structure with some holes where the sunlight came in.

I had really made it. It was almost like a shock when I realized it worked. My emotions changed between infinite joy, humble pride, and enormous relief. I was the first person who had accessed time travel and survived. I needed some tearful minutes to digest this experience mentally. At this moment, my brain ignited a firework of superpositive emotions, which was almost too much for me.

Slowly I regained my emotions, and my training kicked in. I started checking the time machine. The computer showed no error; all batteries were recharged, with the energy provided by the back jump from the fifth to the fourth dimension. I could still smell the ozone and feel the heat created by this enormous amount of energy needed to make this time jump through the dimensions. I deactivated the auto-jump-back device since the main computer did not show any problems. Since this device was introduced for safety reasons, if I had been unconscious or seriously harmed and could not deactivate this device, the time machine would have jumped back to my start date, time, and location. I was all right, so there was no need for this device.

I opened my helmet, removed my safety belt, and stood up, still weak from the past moments. The air in the cave was still full of dust because of the sudden appearance of the time machine. I walked around the time machine to check for damages. There were none. Then I looked through the cave's openings and recognized the hilly area that I had visited during one of my stays in Israel. Now I knew for sure that the time machine worked correctly.

I didn't do much anymore that day. I moved my camping equipment out of the designated locker and assembled a desk and a chair. Then I prepared a meal and some tea using a butane burner, camping cooking and eating equipment, bottled water, and bags of freeze-dried food as it used from astronauts. It was strange to eat this kind of food used by the astronauts today while I was at the time of Jesus. After finishing my meal, I assembled my little tent and prepared my place to sleep with a floor mat and a sleeping bag in the tent. It was much cozier to sleep in my little tent than in the cave itself. Finally, I checked the cave for snakes and scorpions. Then I cleaned the dishes, brushed my teeth, took off my clothes, and jumped into my sleeping bag. I wanted to think about this special day and what happened. However, I was so tired that I could not prevent myself from falling asleep instantly.

My first day after arrival
Final preparations for my journey to Capernaum

The following day, I woke up at dawn and needed some time to realize where I was. The air had an unknown but pleasant scent of flowers. I heard the wind blowing over the rocks, the flying insects, small animals running around, and water flowing through small creeks. Not a single noise of a car, a machine, an aircraft, or anything else artificial. I decided to enjoy these sounds for a while before I stood up to leave my little tent. The air in the cave was chilly, so I put on my modern clothing first. Then I dared to make the first few steps out of the cave. It was a sunny morning. There was a blue sky with some little clouds and a little wind blowing. A limestone formation surrounded me, with many single rocks of different sizes but almost the same color. Here and there, I could spot a green area with yellow-and-orange flowers growing. The air was dry and fresh. After a while, I went back into my cave and prepared a breakfast like the meal I had the night before.

After breakfast, I cleaned the dishes, cleaned my teeth, and washed myself with the bottled water. Then I began with the preparations for my journey to the city of Capernaum. I filled my ancient bags with everything I considered useful and necessary: first aid kit with antivenom for snakebites, spare clothes, money, food, and sandals. Then I filled the waterskin with bottled water and laid my walking stick on top of all this. Then I studied the map to memorize my way, which was as follows: Qumran Caves → Jericho → Bethany → Jerusalem → Bethel → Lebonah → Sychar → Sebaste → Ginae → Nein → Tiberias → Heptapegon → Capernaum. I estimated about fourteen days of walking to cover these trips. With some luck, I could meet Jesus or maybe speak with people who had seen Him or even met Him. Of course, I had some worries about what would lie ahead of me, but having the chance to see or speak to Jesus wiped away all worries about the journey I was about to begin.

After finishing all the preparations, I went out of the cave for a first and brief orientation. I walked some hundred yards around this hilly area to find a way down without the need to climb. It took me a while to find it because it was hidden behind big rocks. At the beginning, it was not easy to walk, but finally, I ended up on a suitable way down the caves. Walking to the city of Jericho would not take more than three to four hours. Finally, I controlled everything I wanted to take with me the next day, like clothing, sandals, my ancient back bag, and waterskin. Then I had a last modern meal as I had it before, cleaned the dishes, and made myself ready for bed. I entered my little tent for the last time to sleep early because I wanted to start the next day shortly after dawn.

Day one of my journey to Capernaum

The next morning, I woke up at dawn. This time, my breakfast was only a cup of tea, two figs, and some nuts. Then I washed myself using bottled water, cleaned my teeth, and put on my ancient clothes and sandals. Because I was afraid to forget something important, for the last time, I controlled my belongings I wanted to take with me. I took my waterskin, made some test walks to optimize the weight of my ancient bag, and checked the height of my walking stick. The last step in this cave was to seal the time machine so nobody could either use it, damage it, or steal it. I stepped out of the cave, which was now my hidden headquarters and my back-to-home station. Then I sealed the cave's entry with heavy stones and camouflaged the entrance of the cave with some bushes.

My destination on this day was the city of Jericho, which I could easily reach in four hours. Jericho was the deepest city globally, about three hundred meters below sea level. Before finding a suitable path to walk, I first went through a rocky and hilly area. The area was barely covered with grass, wildflowers, and low-growing shrubs and trees. There was almost no vegetation. Since the caves lay on sea level and Jericho lay much deeper, my way slowly went down to the level of Jericho. After a while, I saw the first group of about ten people walking toward Jerusalem, in the opposite direction—bearded men and women of different ages. Some women carried their babies in a wrapped baby carrier. There was no significant difference between men's and women's clothing except the headgear. The women wore a kind of veil to hide their faces and hair. The men wore headgear—large square pieces of woolen cloth specially folded and held in place by cord circlets. They talked and laughed, and when they passed me, they greeted me in Hebrew with "Shalom" ("Peace to you"). I then greeted back. I used the chance and asked them when I would reach the city of Jericho, and they answered that I would reach my destination at the late evening. Because I saw the need for a place to sleep, I asked them about a place to sleep overnight; and they recommended a house at the east end of the marketplace, which belonged to the group leader's son-in-law. He told me his name—Samuel—which I should mention at arrival to get a better price per night. I blessed him for this offer, and we continued our journey.

Slowly I found my own walk pace, and the walking stick helped me not to slip. My endurance training paid off now, and it was no problem to continue my trip. After two hours, I saw a group of trees standing around some rocks, where I stopped for a short rest. I drank some water out of my wineskin and ate slowly two figs. I looked at all these people who traveled to Jericho or Jerusalem during my short rest. For me, it was like visiting an oriental museum. I studied the clothing, tried to understand what they spoke in their languages, and observed the people's behavior. Many had livestock (like sheep, goats, chicken, and geese), and some were riding camels. Most impressive was seeing Roman soldiers marching to Jerusalem with their leading officer on horseback at the front.

After about half an hour, I continued my journey; and after a while, I saw the city of Jericho deep in a valley, surrounded by a partly destroyed double wall. Jericho had been founded as an oasis because it was the only place with a well that could provide water for many people. Historians said Jericho was the oldest city globally, which was occupied by twenty-eight civilizations. I stopped and tried to breathe in this ancient view, which I knew well from books but had never before encountered in person. The houses fitted perfectly into the space of the inner walls, and the space between the walls was used by military buildings and people. The walls fitted perfectly into the given valley. I estimated the city's size between two thousand and four thousand citizens.

I enter the ancient city of Jericho the first time

Slowly I reached the city of Jericho. The scene was exciting; many caravans rested before the city's main entrance. They all brought different types of merchandise, like livestock, wood, bricks, salt, fabric, food, etc., into the town. (I remember the smell at this place, which was a combination of human sweat, animal droppings, spices of a different kind, the smoke from the countless campfires, and the many cookshops.) This conglomerate of humans (who spoke many languages), cattle, sheep, goats, camels, and goods from different types built almost its own city.

Slowly I made my way through the crowd to the main gate, always watching my steps and avoiding stepping into animal dung. Four Roman soldiers and one officer guarded the gate. Their uniforms were made from brown leather, shiny body armor with shoulder plates, a metal helmet, groin protection, a big shield, a small dagger, and a big sword—everything close to what we learned in school about Roman soldiers. Their appearance was good enough to suppress any trouble. They checked people for weapons, and since I had none, they let me pass.

After I passed two gates (there were two walls), I got the first impression of the inner part of Jericho. The mainly single-level buildings were squeezed into the space given by the inner wall. These houses had a wooden frame filled with a clay-and-straw mixture. The windows were open and not very big. The roofs were flat and included long wooden beams to improve stability and carrying capacity. All houses were painted in bright colors to reflect the daylight. The construction style of the houses reminded me of typical Mediterranean. On the roof of some buildings, I saw pergolas, which were used as extended living space.

This street, which was the main street, led me to the marketplace, where a lot of trade happened. Farmers sold their livestock, chicken, geese, vegetables, and fruits. I could not identify all, but I saw beans, tomatoes, apples, and pears. Fishermen offered fresh and dried fish. Butchers sold meat from different animals—cattle, goats, and sheep. Flies flew all around the meat because there were no cooling systems, so it was pretty different from marketplaces nowadays. Daily goods like pottery, fabric, knives, shoes, firewood, spices, and herbs were also offered. Because of these bad hygienic conditions, I considered that I would eat only cooked food.

The cookshops there solved my lunch problem. Mainly women and enslaved people were customers in these different shops. Soldiers patrolled around to prevent thefts and fraud. The central building was a temple. This temple was a gigantic building; it was sixty feet tall, forty feet wide, and roughly one hundred feet deep. I stood on the foundation, which was ten feet high. At the front, there was a large wooden door; and at the left and right side stood a column, both of which reached the ceiling. The entire temple was made of limestone. Large steps went from the ground to the entrance of the temple.

I could watch all these people endlessly, but I had to organize my accommodation first. According to the person I had spoken with on my way to Jericho, this house was easy to find at the market's east end. Thus, I looked around and found it. The building had two levels. I knocked at the door and entered the building, and a slave guided me to his master, the building owner. I introduced myself and mentioned his father-in-law, Samuel, whom I had met on my way to Jericho. This name changed the owner's entire behavior, and he gave me his best room for one week at an affordable price. The room itself was simple compared to our modern standards, but it was perfect for me.

The sleeping place was a rectangle on the floor, covered with a thick one-foot-high layer of fresh straw. A small table, a chair, a shelf, and a simple nightstand were all the furniture. A towel, a ceramic wash pan, and a mug of water were free.

There was even a latrine that belonged to this house. The people had to sit on wooden boards with holes, which covered one big trench. Water ran in a big ditch at the people's feet. This was a blessing because there was no need to use the public latrine, which was often a source of many diseases.

I took the chance, locked the door of my room, and prepared my bed for a short nap to refresh myself a little bit after this trip. It was bizarre; one day ago, I was in my time, and now I would become a witness of Jesus's life. This was still overwhelming. I was more exhausted than expected and didn't wake up until the next day.

How I met Mary Magdalene

I was not used to sleeping on a straw bed, so I stood up with stiff muscles. I used the given water to wash my face, then used the latrine the first time, which was strange because there was no privacy in the men's area. Then I went back into my room, washed my hands, grabbed my walking stick, and visited the marketplace for a meal. After a short stroll through the market and evaluating the different cookshops, I concluded it would be best to eat only cooked food. My first breakfast was then something like a burrito—rolled bread with a cooked vegetable paste—and a cup of red wine.

On my way back to my room, a woman suddenly shouted a loud shout: "Oh my god, somebody help me! A snake bit my son! Help! Help!"

The crowd in front of me opened, and I saw a woman kneeling on the ground, holding the hand of a young boy. The snake was still nearby and ready to attack again. I used my walking stick and smashed the snake's head because I wanted to prevent a second attack. After being sure the snake was dead, I identified it as a deadly viper because of its stocky body, wide head, and long, hinged fangs at the front of its mouth. Then I introduced myself as Joshua. The boy needed immediate medical help to prevent him from dying. I felt the crowd begin to become curious. Thus, I told the woman to follow me, carrying the boy to my room. The woman obeyed my wishes, and I knew she was still in shock.

When we arrived at my room, I laid the boy on the floor and told the woman that I was a holistic healer from Alexandria. Then I washed my hands, cleaned the boy's wound, grabbed one of my bags with the medical equipment, and began to pray. I did this to distract the woman from my primary treatment, the push of the injection of the snake antivenom, which I had brought with me. After this, I diligently controlled the breath and pulse of the boy. He had a fever, his pain let him moan, and his entire body shook while his body fought against death. After several hours, I knew that he would survive, but he would need some days to fully recover.

The silent woman sat in the chair and watched what I did during my treatment. Then she asked me, "Who are you, and why are you helping me?"

I answered, "I am Joshua, a holistic healer from Alexandria. My headmaster sent me into this area to study how the illnesses are treated here. At the beginning of our education, holistic healers have to swear an oath to help everyone in need of our help. And I knew your son needed immediate help. Otherwise, he would have died. The only thing I can tell you now is that your son will make it. However, he will need some weeks to recover."

When she heard that her son would survive, she began to weep, feeling lucky and relieved. Then she took hold of both of my hands and said, "Thank you, Joshua. I will be in your debt forever."

I told her she would owe me nothing. Then I asked her, "What's your name, and where is your place of living?"

She answered me, "They call me Mary Magdalene, and this is my ten-year-old son, Nathan. The owner of this building gave me the job to clean the rooms and, therefore, gave my son and me a room in this house. It's no luxury room, but my son and I have a place to live."

Since her son was still sleeping, I asked her to show me her room. She stood up, left the room, and went down the staircase to the first floor. There was a second staircase, and that led into the foundation of the building. The room Mary Magdalene shared with her son was a little bigger than mine. But there were no windows at all, and two oil lamps produced a cozy light.

She said, "It covers the needs. There are even two places to sleep made with straw for my son and me." Suddenly she hugged me intensely and tried to pull me down to her sleeping place, and I was surprised and asked her about the reason.

She just said to me, "You saved my son, and that's the least I can do." At this moment, I realized how beautiful Mary Magdalene was. She was about five feet and six inches tall. A colorful cord closed her outer garment in a way that I could see that she had all the attributes of a well-endowed woman, lovely hips and full bust, which I liked very much. Her hazelnut-brown hair had small curls and framed her face nicely. Her deep-brown eyes, her nose, and her mouth were flawless and showed the softness of a young mother. I guessed her age to be in the midtwenties.

It was a tempting situation, but I didn't want to alter the time line. I told her there was no need to do this and that my oath as a healer prohibited accepting such an offer.

She looked into my eyes, hugged me again, and kissed me on my cheek.

I told her I would move her son into this room. Meanwhile, she should organize a big jar of water and some food. The water would help her son fight the snake venom and help the antivenom work.

I took the sleeping son from my room back into her room and covered him with a blanket. Some minutes later, Mary returned with a big jar of water, some bread, and two dried fish.

I never forgot the real reason for my travel, so I thought, *Why not ask her about Jesus?* I asked her, "Mary, as I told you, the headmaster of my university sent me into this area to study how the people here heal certain illnesses. I want to ask you whether you have ever heard about Jesus of Nazareth, the son of Joseph the carpenter and Mary?"

She began to laugh, and skeptically she asked me, "Have you made this long trip from Alexandria to Jericho to see Jesus of Nazareth? I had no idea the reputation of our town character goes that far."

I was surprised because I heard some irony in her answer. I answered her, "Yes, we heard some good stories about Jesus in Alexandria, but tell me about Him. Maybe He is not the right one."

So she told me, "Years ago He was a good-looking, hard-working smart guy, but then about a half year ago, He completely changed. He told everybody He was the son of God and would become the world's savior. Nobody believed Him. People began to mock Him. Over time, He lost every job, began to drink, and became homeless. Every once in a while, when He needs money, He helps clean the public latrines."

Now it was on me to look astonished, and I thought maybe it was a different person! So I asked her whether it might be possible to help me meet Jesus tomorrow.

She said, "Yes," still shaking her head in disbelief over what I wanted from Him.

So I wished her a good night, gave her final medical advice for her son's treatment, and told her that if anything would turn up strange, she could wake me up, even in the middle of the night. Then I went back to my room. I washed my face, made myself ready, and went to bed with really strange thoughts about the next day, when I would see the real, living Jesus. How would this be?

How I met Jesus the first time

I woke up the following day, washed myself, and went out of the house for breakfast. When I came back, I met Mary Magdalene in the middle of her job duties (she cleaned empty rooms for new guests, replaced the straw, and swept the floor), and she told me she would be finished in the early afternoon. I asked her about her son's well-being; and she said he woke up in the morning and ate a little but then continued sleeping—a good sign of recovery. I told her that she could knock on my door when we could meet Jesus.

She said yes with a strange smile on her face.

I went back into my room and sat down on my chair. My thoughts began to go wild. What if this Jesus I was looking for was the divine Jesus, the only Son of God? The Jesus of the New Testament? This Jesus should be the town character, a drunk, and a cleaner of public latrines. I couldn't believe this!

I used the remaining time to sleep a few hours. Mary Magdalene knocked on my door in the early afternoon, as she had promised. She told me that she had asked some friends about the whereabouts of Jesus. They had told her of a barn where He typically slept overnight. I put on my sandals, and Mary Magdalene led me to this barn.

The barn stood in the city's outer areas near the inner wall. We reached it after a long and stressful walk through the entire city. When we came to the barn, we met the owner. He was a dark-skinned, dusty, dirty, and bald-headed man and looked not very trustworthy. When we asked him about Jesus, he walked with us to a corner in the barn; and there we found the sleeping Jesus, who lay on a pile of straw. His appearance was terrible because His clothing was dirty, severely torn, had an offensive smell, and His scent was horrible.

I touched his side several times with my left foot to wake him up.

After a while, He woke up and looked around. He looked confused, and He needed a bit to realize that we stood in front of Him. With slow movements and visual trouble, He stood up and looked at us. Then he recognized Mary Magdalene and said the words "Hello, Mary. What gives me after all the past time the honor of your visit, and how is Nathan doing?"

She answered him, "Thanks for asking. Nathan is doing well. The reason for my visit is this man, Joshua, and he came from Alexandria to see You."

Then Jesus turned around and looked into my eyes, and I in His. At this moment, I knew that yes, this was Jesus, the Son of God.

He asked me, "Joshua, I am honored to get a visitor from Alexandria, but what can I do for you?"

I asked him, "Are you Jesus of Nazareth, son of Joseph and Mary? Was your mother a virgin when she conceived you from the Lord? Have you been confirmed in the temple of Jerusalem at the age of twelve? Has God, your Father, given you a task that seems impossible to do?"

It looked like every one of my questions was a punch in His stomach. Slowly He turned His body to me with clenched fists; He looked like a cornered wounded tiger ready to strike.

My fight with Jesus

When I looked at Him, my martial arts education immediately kicked in. I had a man in front of me who was desperate and scared. Then suddenly He attacked me, punched me in my face, grabbed me, and pushed me with an unexpected force through the barn. I counterattacked him with all my power, so our fight became tough.

He shouted at me, *"Who are you? Has My Father sent you to Me to go after Me? Do you know what My Father wants Me to do? Have you ever tried to walk in My shoes?"*

Meanwhile, we fought like wild bulls; punch followed punch, and kick followed kick. After a while, I found that Jesus became weaker. He was going to have breathing problems. The color of His face changed to deep red. So I landed a lucky punch in His face that sent Him into dreamland, and He fell to the ground.

Mary Magdalene, who witnessed the entire fight, was upset because she had no idea why we fought. I took care of Jesus, grabbed a bucket of water, poured the water over His face and body, knelt by Him, and helped Him stand up. Then I poured a bucket of water over myself to refresh myself and filled it again at the barn's well to drink the water.

Then it was on me to kneel before Him with the words "Lord, forgive me. I have failed. Violence is normally not my way, but I had no choice."

Jesus laid both His hands on my shoulders and said to me, "Joshua, My friend, you fought well!"

Mary Magdalene was even more surprised about our behavior and shouted at me, *"Are you crazy?* First, you punched Jesus to hell, and then you knelt in front of Him and addressed Him as Lord?"

I tried to calm her down, which was not so easy, and I promised her I would explain everything when the time was right.

Jesus tells me about His life and struggle in Jericho

We found a place in the barn, near a forge, where all three of us could sit.

After a while of silence, Jesus began to speak, "Joshua, I owe you an explanation about My behavior, and you have deserved it. I don't know what Mary Magdalene told you about Me, so I will tell you the story of My life for the last twelve years. At age eighteen, I left My parents to make My own living. My knowledge and experience as a carpenter, which My father, Joseph, had taught me, was good enough to make this step. I settled here in Jericho because a carpenter with a good reputation wanted to hand over his business to a younger man, and nobody in his family wanted this job. I spoke with him, and he gave me the chance to work for him for about a year.

"In this time, I learned even more, especially the business side. He was convinced he could hand over his business to Me when the time was over. We made a contract, and I agreed to pay him a fixed amount as long as he lived. So far, everything went well, and I fell in love with a woman. You can guess who this was. Yes, it was Mary Magdalene. I asked her to stay with Me, and she said yes. After a while, she got pregnant, and Nathan was born. We were a lucky family, and I tried to be a good husband.

"Then, nine years after Nathan's birth, my heavenly Father reminded Me about my duty, and who can go against the will of God? Since then, I have known that I am God's Son, and My purpose is to save the sinners from this world. However, I will be crucified and die for doing this, and three days later, I will return from the dead."

When Mary Magdalene heard this, she said, "Not again with this nonsense. I can't believe it. Joshua, when Jesus began to speak about His duty in public, the people began to think He was insane. We lost all customers, and it was sheer luck that the former owner released us from the business contract without harm. But we lost all our income. Jesus was a responsible husband, so the only way to protect Nathan and me was to send us away." Mary Magdalene began to cry bitterly when she told me this.

First steps to support Jesus

After Mary Magdalene finished, I needed to think about all this. I concluded that we should stop and continue tomorrow under better conditions. I said to both, "Jesus and Mary Magdalene, I am honored that you told me all this, and I have to think about what can be done. So for today, I think it is better to stop here because I need some time to digest what I have heard. Today, more important will be to make You a suitable man again, Jesus. So, Mary Magdalene, since Jesus is still your husband, you should still know the size of His clothing. I guess you know a place where you can get new clothing and new sandals, the normal ones, nothing fancy. I give you five denarii. Is this enough? But before doing this, Jesus, You should wash and go to a barber to fix Your beard. Is there a place in this town to do this?"

Mary Magdalene answered with relief, "Since we are still a couple, I will take Jesus with me and do all you have said. It will take a while, and you can wait in your room and have some rest there. I will knock at your door when we are ready."

I agreed. Mary Magdalene and Jesus went away, and I strolled back to my room, having many thoughts about Jesus and Mary Magdalene in my head.

When I reached the house, I asked for the owner. After some time, the owner appeared and asked me what he could do for me. I told him that my stay would be one week longer and that I would like to rent a room for a guest simultaneously. He told me yes but that it would be a little bit more expensive. I agreed and paid the rent for both rooms immediately. Then the homeowner showed me the room, which was next to mine. I was fully satisfied and went back into my room. I lay down on my bed to recover a little from this tiring day.

After some time, it was almost dusk. Somebody knocked on my door, and I answered, "Come in."

It was Jesus with no terrible smell, nicely and neatly dressed and properly shaved, as He should be. I stood up and looked at Him. He stood at about six feet tall, was dressed in a light-gray garment, and had dark-brown straight hair to His shoulders. The color of His face was some kind of dark ocher. His face was oval, His beard about two inches long, His lips thin, and His nose long. Most interesting were His oval brown eyes because when I looked at His eyes, I had the feeling I was looking into an infinite universe.

I said to Him, "Jesus, now You look like the Son of God, and don't worry about the money. And I guess Mary Magdalene takes care of Nathan."

Then He answered me, "I thank you for what you have done for Me. It can only be repaid in heaven. And thank you for what you did for Nathan. Without your help, he would've been dead."

Then there was a knock at the door, and Mary Magdalene entered the room. She said, "Nathan is doing well, and now I can recognize my husband as such again."

I told her, "You did an excellent job, and this shows me that you are still in love with Jesus." Then I said to them that I had rented the room next to my room for Jesus for the same time as I would be here. This would be all for today, and we would continue tomorrow after dawn.

They both thanked me again for what I did and the room for Jesus. Then they left my room, and I made myself ready for bed. I wanted to think about all that had happened, but I fell asleep immediately.

Joshua realizes that God has sent him to Jesus

The following day, I woke up right before dawn, stood up, washed myself, and put my clothes and sandals on. Then Jesus knocked on my door, and I welcomed Him. I offered Him the chair to sit on, but He preferred to sit on the floor. And so did I. We looked silently at each other.

Jesus began to speak, "From My birth on, I was told I am the Son of God, that I would become the savior of all souls in the world who believe in me, and that I am the founder of the new covenant. All this would finally cost Me my earthly life, and I would resurrect from the dead and ascend to heaven, where I will meet God, my Father. These are the things I was told. For Me, this was a shock. Before this, I felt like an ordinary man. I ignored and suppressed it for many years.

"I almost forgot it, but one year ago, all this was told Me again in a dream. My Father in heaven reminded Me in this dream what My task here on earth is and that I should start it within the next couple of years. It was a punch in My stomach because I was the luckiest man in the world before the event, with a beloved wife, a healthy son, and a good-going business.

"After this, I lost control of My life and everything else, including My wife and My son. I felt sorry for Mary Magdalene because she never believed this and found herself now as the wife of a man who became insane overnight. And yesterday, Joshua, you appeared here, asking the right questions as if this would be normal. Strangely, you healed Nathan from a deadly snakebite, and you knew in a few hours that he would survive. There is no known cure for this type of injury as far as I know!

"Joshua, to be honest, I know who you are, where you come from, and that you are a true believer in Me. Well, Joshua, I think My Father in heaven supported you with godly help to find Me and help Me start My ministry!"

Now it was my turn to be astonished. It never crossed my mind that God directed me through all the past project time to finally support Jesus, His Son! I was stunned! Overall these twelve years, I was a servant of the Lord without realizing this!

I answered Jesus, "Yes, my Lord, You are right. I came from the future, AD 2022, and I am a time traveler. I needed twelve years to develop a time-travel machine and prepare myself to travel through the time to find and talk with You, my Lord."

After I admitted my real identity, there was silence in the room, and I thought my confirmation of Jesus's prediction also stunned Jesus itself.

The truth begins to reveal itself

A knock at my door interrupted the silence in my room, and I answered with "Come in."

Mary Magdalene apparently had been at the market because she brought a basketful of food for breakfast.

I told her, "Good morning, Mary Magdalene. I see you are a person who can take care of others. How is Nathan? Has he had breakfast too?"

Then she answered, "Good morning, my friends. I had some money left yesterday, and I thought it might be good to purchase this food for breakfast and maybe eat the leftovers for lunch. And yes, Nathan is doing well, and I had a small breakfast with him this morning."

Then we took some food out of the basket and shared it with one another. There was flatbread, dried fish, figs, a paste made from vegetables, and a jar of wine. Then again, there was silence in the room, but eating meals caused it this time.

When the meal was over, Mary Magdalene asked me, "What will we do on this day?"

Now it was on me to answer her. "Mary Magdalene, do you know somebody who can take care of Nathan the next two days? I will show you something about which I can't speak before you have seen it, for safety reasons. We three will go to the caves of Qumran, which means four to five hours on foot until we reach the caves, and trust me, there I will answer all questions that you have now. We will need some food, but we have plenty here and some water for us for three days. Mary Magdalene, don't be afraid. Just trust me and don't ask any questions now. When we are there, you can ask whatever you want. How much time would we need for preparation? It would be nice to reach the caves at dusk."

Jesus stayed calm.

Mary Magdalene just said, "So be it! I will make arrangements for Nathan and leave him some food here. I have to tell the landlord that I will be away for two days for an important private business. I think we can start soon in the afternoon to reach the caves in time."

Jesus and I agreed. So they went back to their rooms and prepared themselves for this day trip.

We started shortly after noon, left the city behind us, and began the steep way to the caves. We had a lot of company this way because it was the only way to and from Jericho. Some had livestock, from single persons to groups of people, and one group used oxen to pull a wagon loaded with cargo. Sometimes we had some small talk with these travelers about their well-being and exchanged the latest news, sometimes even jokes. After a while, we reached the place where I had rested a few days before. We rested there again and used the time to drink some water and eat some bread with vegetable paste. Then we continued our trip. After a short time, we left the normal path and continued traveling to the Qumran caves.

It was almost dusk when we reached my cave. I told both Jesus and Mary Magdalene that they should not be afraid of whatever they would see then. I removed the bushes and tiny rocks that camouflaged the cave entry and entered the cave. The first thing I had to do was disable the time machine's protection unit to prevent self-destruction. Both Jesus and Mary Magdalene looked at the time machine with an expression of astonishment.

Jesus gets help for His ministry from a higher force, and Mary Magdalene realizes the truth

Now all three of us stood in front of the time machine. Then Mary Magdalene began slowly, with open eyes, to move toward the time machine, and finally, she carefully touched it. Then she turned to me and asked, "Joshua, what is this? I have never ever seen such an apparatus in my entire life! It is crafted in a way unknown to me, and believe me, I have seen a lot in my life. I came around! I think not even the Romans could build such a machine. It looks like something not from this world!"

I answered her, "Mary Magdalene, you are closer to the truth than you may think. My real name is Joshua, but I don't come from Alexandria. I am a time traveler who comes from the future about 2,000 years from now and from a country which you don't know because it will be discovered in 1,500 years from now. I am a scientist who wanted to see and speak with Jesus for reasons I will explain later.

"I know this is hard to believe, but don't forget I saved Nathan from a viper snakebite. Jesus told me that He never saw a person walking away alive after such an attack. And He is right. In your time, I know there is no cure available. This cure will be developed in about 1,900 years!"

Then Mary Magdalene answered, "Well, to be honest, this puzzled me as well, but it was the life of my son Nathan that you saved. And therefore, I considered not to ask. And tell me, Joshua. So all your people can travel through time?"

I answered her, "No, I needed about twelve years to develop this time machine. This is the prototype, and I may destroy it to prevent misuse when my goal is reached. But let me show you more of this machine." I showed them the gigantic battery, the dimension generator, the primary control units, and more. During the tour through the time machine, I took my butane burner and some of my modern type of food to offer later to both of my guests. Then I grabbed my folding table and three folding chairs and unfolded them to have a more comfortable place. Then I told Mary Magdalene to put the food on the table.

Meanwhile, I brought out silverware, plates, drinking glasses, and bottled water from my time-machine storage. Then I prepared and warmed up my dehydrated food until it was ready to be eaten. After all this was done, I invited both to sit down and have dinner.

I asked Mary Magdalene if she would have believed me to be a time traveler without seeing this time machine. She said no, but now she believed me after seeing the entire machine. Then I asked Jesus, "Jesus, do You believe now that Your Father in heaven, with all His power, guided and supported me over these many years to bring the time machine to a successful end, to make it possible that I could visit and help You?"

Jesus said, "Yes, I must admit that I am impressed that My Father in heaven found you, Joshua, who is capable and willing to take the time machine to make this happen. You are here, which gives Me something back, something I lost many years ago. I can trust My Father, who lives in heaven, because He loves me unconditionally. I know my destiny will be hard, and finally, the Romans will crucify Me. But it will be for the common good. I will save all sinners who believe in Me."

Then Mary Magdalene asked Jesus, "And what will be with us, our relationship, and Nathan?"

He hugged her intensely with tears in His eyes and answered her, "Mary Magdalene, between us nothing will change. I promise you will be My earthly love forever, but we must be careful due to the circumstances. I will have many enemies, and I don't want you or Nathan to be endangered. Therefore, in public, we are just good friends, nothing more. I am sure there will be ways to live our love. You will be My earthly support till my end, as My Father in heaven will be My spiritual support, and I need both of you for Me to fulfill My destiny. So right now, there is only one thing left for me to do!"

Jesus prays to His Father in heaven and gets His blessing

Jesus stood up from his chair and told us to follow Him. We went out of the cave and climbed to the top of the cave, which was not easy because meanwhile, it had become night and I could see almost nothing. But Jesus told us to trust and follow him. Finally, we reached the top, where Jesus commanded us to wait until He would call us. So we waited quite a while until suddenly a shining cloud came down from heaven and wrapped the kneeling Jesus. It was the most beautiful thing I had ever seen in my entire life. We could see Jesus praying and talking in this cloud. Then, after a while, He invited Mary Magdalene and me to come and told us that there was no reason to be afraid. So we both went slowly toward this shiny cloud until we touched it. What I felt at this moment was almost indescribable. This cloud was filled with unconditional love and endless harmony, something I would never ever want to leave. Then somehow, because of these overwhelming emotions, I lost my consciousness.

The final breakfast with Jesus and Mary Magdalene

I woke up the following day in the cave and looked around, and Jesus was there. He had prepared breakfast, and Mary Magdalene helped Him. I stood up slowly and said, "Good morning, Jesus and Mary Magdalene. How are you both on this wonderful day?"

Then Jesus said, "Joshua, My friend, indeed, it is a beautiful day. Let's sit down and have some breakfast, and then we can talk about what happened last night."

Apparently, they had found the food I brought with me, and even the tea was available. So we silently ate a delicious breakfast of bread, nuts, figs, and dried fruits.

Then Jesus began to speak, "Joshua, what you have seen yesterday night was the Holy Spirit, the connection between My Father in heaven and Me here on earth. We use it to communicate by praying. Thanks to you and Mary Magdalene, I have accepted My divine destiny, and My Father has blessed Me to be ready for this. His blessing also gave Me the strength, wisdom, love, and divine power to do this. I invited you to come and touch the Holy Spirit to give you an idea of what this might be and what your soul will encounter in heaven after you die. I will be in your debt forever because you made My way possible."

Then we were silent for a while. I asked Jesus how we would proceed.

He said, "Mary Magdalene and I will return to Jericho, and we will leave you here, Joshua. Mary Magdalene, Nathan, and I will leave Jericho as soon as possible and travel to the city of Capernaum. You know why!"

Hearing this was a little shock for me, but I knew that as long as I stayed in the past, the risk of damaging the time line would be higher. So there was little more to do for me except one thing.

I asked Mary Magdalene to come with me. She followed me into the storage area of my time machine. Here I opened the safe, which contained the silver denarii. I took half of these, put them into a small purse, and handed it over to the surprised Mary Magdalene with the words "You will need them more than I do!"

While Jesus and Mary Magdalene prepared themselves for their return to Jericho, my heart became really sad, and tears began to fill my eyes. First, I hugged Mary Magdalene and wished her luck and patience with Jesus. Then I turned to Jesus. We looked into each other's eyes, then we hugged intensely. We both had tears in our eyes.

Then Jesus said, "Thank you, My friend. Joshua, you have no idea what you did! When the time comes, we will meet again in heaven."

Then we shook hands for the final farewell. They both left my cave. I followed both for a few yards and stopped then; and then they turned back to me, waved their hands one last time, and continued their way back to Jericho.

The end

Then I was alone in my cave. I tried to handle my emotions and memories about the last couple of days. It was almost too much for me. I sat down on a chair and let my feelings fill my eyes with tears. My wish to meet and speak to Jesus had been fulfilled. This had happened in a way that I had never expected. God had supported me with the development of the time machine, and I had, had no idea about this. Ironically, my time travel was part of the natural history, which meant the development and building of the time machine were never in danger because I was supposed to visit and support Jesus anyway. This meant it had been part of my destiny ever since! I had not changed the history, and everything that happened had never been recorded. So nobody would know about me.

The question now was "What should I do?" I could jump around with the time machine in history. Should I go back into my normal space-time? Destroy the time machine and end my life? What would be next?

To be continued…

About the Author

Peter Krause, born in 1963 in Germany, worked and lived for about fifty years in Germany. He worked as a software development engineer for more than thirty years. During this time, he never developed strong connections to the Lord. At age fifty, he immigrated to Tennessee, USA. He joined the St. John's Episcopal Church and the EfM Group in Johnson City, Tennessee. His colleagues at work and the EfM Group in Johnson City, Tennessee, supported him, and he slowly found his way back to the Lord. Because of his struggle between engineering and faith, he wrote this story.

www.ingramcontent.com/pod-product-compliance
Lightning Source LLC
Chambersburg PA
CBHW031003180726
47993CB00018B/1534